Merlin the Mouse

by Jackie Walter and Spike Maguire

W

D0308405

Merlin the mouse lived in a cage.

Mia loved him.

She played with him
and she looked after him.

Mia had a cat, too.

The cat wanted to play
with Merlin.

"Cats can't play with mice!"
said Mia.

"You must look after him.
I will be cross if he gets out."

Mia went to school.

"I want to go out," said Merlin
and he opened the door
of his cage.

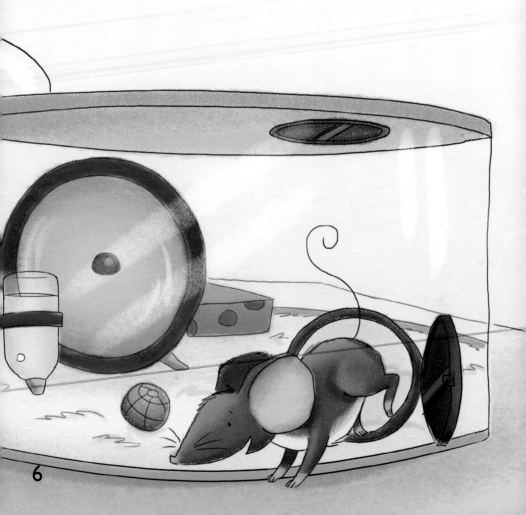

"You can't come out!"

said the cat.

"Yes I can," said Merlin.

Merlin ran across the room.

"You can't go into the hall!"

said the cat.

"Yes I can," said Merlin.

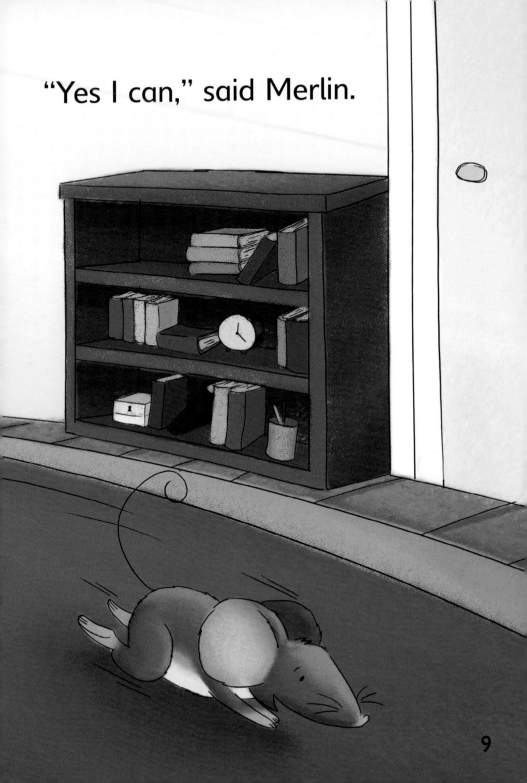

Merlin ran into the hall.

"You can't go down the stairs!"

said the cat.

"Yes I can," said Merlin.

Merlin ran down the stairs.

"You can't go in the kitchen!"

said the cat.

"Yes I can," said Merlin.

Merlin opened the bread bin.

"You can't eat the bread!"

said the cat.

"Yes I can," said Merlin.

"Oh, no!" said the cat.

"Mia will be cross."

Merlin got some bread
and he ran back to his cage.

17

Mia came home from school.

She went to see Merlin.

"Hello Merlin," said Mia.

"Thank you for
looking after him,"
she said to the cat.

Story trail

Start

Start at the beginning of the
story trail. Ask your child to retell
the story in their own words,
pointing to each picture in turn
to recall the sequence of events.

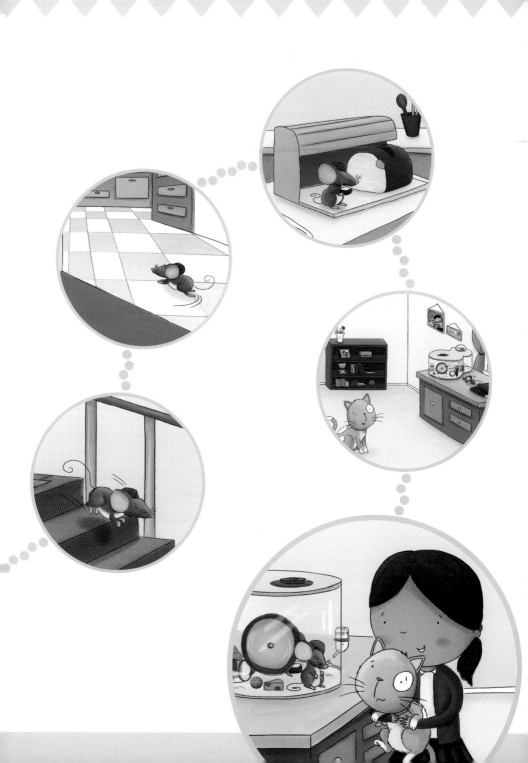

Independent Reading

This series is designed to provide an opportunity for your child to read on their own. These notes are written for you to help your child choose a book and to read it independently.

In school, your child's teacher will often be using reading books which have been banded to support the process of learning to read. Use the book band colour your child is reading in school to help you make a good choice. *Merlin the Mouse* is a good choice for children reading at Blue Band in their classroom to read independently.

The aim of independent reading is to read this book with ease, so that your child enjoys the story and relates it to their own experiences.

About the book

Mia loves her pet mouse, Merlin. When she goes to school, she leaves her cat in charge. But Merlin soon escapes from his cage!

Before reading

Help your child to learn how to make good choices by asking: "Why did you choose this book? Why do you think you will enjoy it?" Look at the cover together and ask: "What do you think the story will be about?" Support your child to think of what they already know about the story context. Read the title aloud and ask: "What is Merlin doing? What do you think the cat is thinking?" Remind your child that they can try to sound out the letters to make a word if they get stuck. Decide together whether your child will read the story independently or read it aloud to you. When books are short, as at Blue Band, your child may wish to do both!

During reading

If reading aloud, support your child if they hesitate or ask for help by telling the word. Remind your child of what they know and what they can do independently.

If reading to themselves, remind your child that they can come and ask for your help if stuck.

After reading

Use the story trail to encourage your child to retell the story in the right sequence, in their own words.

Support comprehension by asking your child to tell you about the story. Help your child think about the messages in the book that go beyond the story and ask: "Why do you think Merlin leaves his cage? Why does the cat get so worried?"

Give your child a chance to respond to the story: "Did you have a favourite part? What else could Merlin have done while Mia was at school?"

Extending learning

In the classroom your child's teacher may be reinforcing punctuation. On a few of the pages, check your child can recognise capital letters, full stops and question marks by asking them to point these out. The teacher may also be reinforcing how words can combine to make sentences and linking clauses using 'and'. Find an example of a connective in the story and ask your child to point to the connecting word (see pages 3, 6 and 16 for examples).

Franklin Watts
First published in Great Britain in 2017
by The Watts Publishing Group

Copyright © The Watts Publishing Group 2017

Series Editors: Jackie Hamley and Melanie Palmer
Series Advisors: Dr Sue Bodman and Glen Franklin
Series Designer: Peter Scoulding

A CIP catalogue record for this book is
available from the British Library.

ISBN 978 1 4451 5481 7 (hbk)
ISBN 978 1 4451 5482 4 (pbk)
ISBN 978 1 4451 6091 7 (library ebook)

Printed in China

Franklin Watts
An imprint of
Hachette Children's Group
Part of The Watts Publishing Group
Carmelite House
50 Victoria Embankment
London EC4Y 0DZ

An Hachette UK Company
www.hachette.co.uk

www.franklinwatts.co.uk

FSC
www.fsc.org
MIX
Paper from
responsible sources
FSC® C104740